1864

Paul Duerr

thepaulseph Publishing

This novella is dedicated to every teacher I have ever had. My respect, admiration, and heartfelt thankfulness cannot be expressed enough.

The following story is historical fiction. It is dedicated to the brave men in blue who fought to preserve the Union in the conflict that changed the course of American History.

CONTENTS

THE AMERICAN CIVIL WAR.

◆ ◆ ◆

"No terms except an unconditional and immediate surrender can be accepted."

-Ulysses S. Grant

◆ ◆ ◆

The main characters, some names, and some aspects of this story are fictional. Some are not. This is historical fiction told from the mind of a 16 year-old boy from New Jersey. This story was written with nothing but respect for History.

PART 1: THE OVERLAND CAMPAIGN

◆ ◆ ◆

LIEUTENANT GENERAL ULYSSES S. GRANT'S UNION ARMY

◆ ◆ ◆

Major General Meade's Army
of the Potomac,
Major General Hancock's II Corps,
Second Division, Fifth Brigade, 69th New
Jersey Volunteer Infantry Regiment,
Major Bill Johnson, Commanding.

CHAPTER 1

4 May 1864, Across the Rapidan
River near Chancellorsville
in the Wilderness.

The rebel army was still reeling from their massive defeats at Gettysburg, Vicksburg, and Chattanooga. Miles of destroyed rail, telegraph lines, and abandoned wagons lined the streets throughout the beleaguered south. Entire towns were converted into hospitals, cities were converted into bastions, and the southern way of life was under siege. Hundreds of thousands lay dead, and the rebels were desperately conscripting any able-bodied man, even more so now with General Grant in charge of the whole Union army. He wasn't like any of the hot-headed Generals before him. He never gave Robert

E. Lee and his conscripts a chance to breathe, always attacking at every turn without retreating, no matter what the cost, and that was the point of this campaign. He knew how to win this war and wasn't afraid to do it. General Grant was willing to butcher hundreds of thousands of his men and set every southern city ablaze until they begged for mercy and waved the white flag over the south and their outdated way of life. So long as the rebels still had a fight in them, we would be on the march to stomp them down.

We were on the march to engage Lee's army just west of the old Chancellorsville battlefield. The Battle of Chancellorsville was widely regarded as Lee's masterpiece. He was able to masterfully outflank and outwit the most professional army in the world with his old men and farmhands. I was at Chancellorsville during the battle as a company commander in the 69th. I served alongside the legendary Captain Deckhart, the commander of the 5th New Jersey Light Artillery, Battery D and a would become numb to physical pain but living in constant mental agony. I feared I was going insane.

We had just crossed the Rapidan River on the way to attack Hill's Corps. He was one of Lee's wing commanders, guarding his right flank. Meade and the rest of the army were further north, attacking Ewell. Grant ordered Hancock south, where we could make sure Grant's left was secure and the rebels right could be attacked. The next morning, we would be in the thick of the action at the front of the line, right where we liked it.

CHAPTER 2

5 May 1864, Southeast of the
Union Line near Chancellorsville
in the Wilderness.

Hancock's entire II Corps was preparing to move against the extreme right of the Rebel Army. The whole Corps was lined up down a road stretching a half mile, with ranks and files spreading into the adjacent forests and woods. The 69th New Jersey was at the front of the advance, armed with m1842 smoothbore Springfield muskets. They could be loaded with buck and ball shot, which was a .69 caliber round ball with. 30 caliber buckshot, and used effectively at close range as a shotgun. Of course, in doing so we'd sustain heavy casualties, but also inflict them doubly so.

Our batteries were lined up two-thousand yards from the enemy, loaded with shell. We knew the rebels were somewhat entrenched and prepared to receive our advance. I had my sword drawn, and I was at the left of the regiment, three companies strong. Company commanders had their swords drawn and were dressing the lines. Men had their arms at the shoulder with socket bayonets attached, ready for a quicktime march into oblivion. All we had to do was wait for the order. Before I knew it, we heard the bugle.

"At the quick time! Forward march!" I yelled.

The whole corps began moving forward into a clearing, with us at the very front. The sound of the bugle faded out as the sounds of drums began to take over the air. There was a hill in front of us and woods all around. It was the worst position I had ever seen.

"Double quick! Forward!" I yelled as the men picked up their pace. The quicker we could get through the clearing, the better.

The men ran until we finally reached the hill and I gave the order to march on the hill. I had a feeling they would be on the other side of the hill. We slowly marched up the side. Men were breathing so heavy it could probably have been heard on the other side, myself included. Our regimental colors were peeking over and were getting higher and higher as we marched to the crest. Before I could rear my head, the rebels unleashed a devastating volley from their fortification that cut down at least two dozen men. Their batteries began to shred the adjacent lines with canister shot. The air filled with the toxic smell of black powder and smoke, rendering visibility a precious luxury. Our own artillery began firing over our heads.

"Forward! Don't stop," I yelled as I raised my sword, "stay in your lines! Do not break!"

We kept marching as the regiments behind us halted on the hill and began volleying the rebel lines. We kept marching forward until we got to a range I liked.

"Halt! At the ready!" Men brought their arms off the shoulder and men repeated the order.

"Take aim!" I shouted. An eerie silence fell on the battlefield, as time seemed to have slowed.

"Fire!" The subsequent volley sent monumental amounts of deadly shrapnel at the hordes of rebels hiding in their trench.

"Reload!" I shouted.

We continued pouring buck and ball into their lines, and they continued sending volleys back to us. Solid shot was landing all around us, blowing holes in our lines. A shot landed directly in front of my line and showered us in red dirt. Projectiles were soaring through the air as if it were a unique architecture in an ancient city. We were shooting at one hundred yards, our shots were showering them in a hail of lead in all directions, but they were sending it back. My second in command, Captain Steven Roberts, was keeping the boys in line, sending a torrent of bullets tearing through the air into the rebels. We eventually had to fall back to our hill and rejoin the main line in standard volleys. Our shots tore through their lines, allowing the rest of the brigade to move up. The line was stretched from one edge of the forest to the other. Men were being shredded where they stood, and gaps were being widened in our line. Soon, the rest of the division moved up and pressed our advantage. General Gibbon was shouting orders between the lines and General Hancock was atop his horse yet again raising morale with his mere presence. The terrible cacophony of musket fire, explosions, and screams had eventually caused the rebels to fall back from their initial fortifications and reinforce their stronger ones to the rear. For now at least, we drove the rebels back and were prepared to fight them again tomorrow.

CHAPTER 3

*6 May 1864, Southeast of the
Union Line near Chancellorsville
in the Wilderness.*

With our distinguished performance the previous day, our regiment received a commendation by General Gibbon, our division commander, and was given the nickname the "Brawling 69th" because of our up-close and personal fighting style. From afar, it looked as if we were the only thing keeping them at bay. An unstoppable Union met an immovable Confederacy, and the Union had prevailed. We do enjoy getting in their face and giving them the cold steel. We were reminiscent of the "Fighting 69th", the 69th New York Infantry Regiment, the infamous fighting Irish of the Irish Brigade.

The Fifth Brigade in Gibbon's Second Division was made up of us -the 69th New Jersey Volunteer Infantry, as well as the 47th New Jersey Volunteer Infantry, the 108th New Jersey Volunteer Infantry, the 32nd Connecticut Volunteer Infantry, the 20th Vermont Volunteer Infantry, and the 2nd Wisconsin Sharpshooters. It was nicknamed the "Bear Brigade" because of our ruthless and merciless combat tactics. We would maul the opposing lines until they fell back or were slaughtered. The Brawling 69th of the Bear Brigade took this to the most extreme. Our brigade commander was Colonel Robert Morely of New Jersey. I knew all of my fellow regimental commanders and got along well with them. They all fought hard and led with the fighting fury of a thousand suns. All of our numbers were low, especially after yesterday's engagement. Notwithstanding the sharpshooters, we all have just under three hundred men per regiment. At this point in the war, sixteen hundred men in a brigade was average. At the start of the war, there would be five thousand at least.

Captain Roberts approached me.

"Sir, beg to report."

"Go on."

"Sir, the situation is very confused. Rebels are still scattered throughout sir. What are your orders?"

"Clear them out, Captain. No quarter." I said sternly as I put on my gloves.

"Yes sir." The regiment cleared the few skirmishers in quick fashion. From afar, the screams and yelps for mercy were silenced by lone gunshots. It sent shivers down my spine.

The division had just advanced past the hill where our artillery was now positioned. We swept the rebels out of their first line and were preparing to advance against their next line. They had the night to reinforce but so did we, and we now had amassed artillery, raining solid shot and percussion all over their lines. Again, we were at the front of the line quick time marching into their abandoned first trench, and, yet again, moving over the top into the line of fire.

"Go get 'em' Brawlers!" yelled a soldier we passed in the line behind us.

"Forward!" I shouted, as mounds of dirt were launched into the air all around us from rebel cannon.

Beyond the abandoned trench was a thick line of trees, and as we marched through we saw their next trench abandoned as well. Suddenly, with artillery still raining down all over us, Confederate General Longstreet's entire elite Corps was advancing towards us. They were not but one hundred yards ahead and stopped to form a line of battle. Thousands of them came pouring out of the thick forest and started forming their battle lines. A massive exchange of artillery was soaring in the air above us. We stretched out to meet their advance as the rest of the brigade moved up in support, and was stretched out in a quarter mile long line. We met their counterattack with hails of hot lead, tearing up their lines. Ripple fire and volley fire rendered the stream of gunshots continuous and devastating. In turn, we were taking unsustainable losses, but we were holding them off long enough for the rest of the division to move up. It was imperative that we held the line and caused as much damage as possible. Our buck and ball was extremely effective at this range. After a while, a small brigade of Texans began to break formation, fix bayonets, and charge our line. Their rebel yell was ear-piercing.

"Bayonets! Countercharge!" I shouted, as I swung my sword.

The boys sent one more volley of buck and ball at them before they ran in beside me and ran their bayonets through the attacking rebels. It was a mess of blood and dust under the burning sun, with fire and gunpowder filling the air. Explosions from artillery had ignited dry timber, engulfing the Wilderness in flames. Smoke encircled the combatants, suffocating them to death, while others burned alive before they could reach the melee action. In the middle of the fight, while I was running my sword through screaming hillbillies and farmers, one of them managed to slash my shoulder and knock me on the ground. I drew my pistol and shot five rebels who ran at me in succession. My head started spinning, and my vision became blurred. The ringing in my ears became louder and louder until finally, the incessant yelling finally came to a slow halt as the beleaguered Texans fell back to their lines. I laid on the ground in the fetal position as men retreated over me. I quickly stood back on my feet and noticed that the 69th New Jersey was the only regiment that countercharged. Behind us the brigade was standing with a regiment sized gap. They were cheering for us as what remained of the regiment reformed and filled the gap. We drove back an entire brigade by ourselves, and our numbers were reduced to just over one hundred fifty. It was not enough to drive back Longstreet, however. As his lines were reorganizing, he dispatched three brigades to flank us from an old railway pass. Sharpshooters were doing their work on the confused rebels. They were apparently doing very good work, as we were informed he was severely wounded in the neck, but his Corps was still on the advance. We were sent to the rear of the line as the division fell back under the pressure of Longstreet's counterattack. They attacked again around 4pm, but they had not committed a substantial force, and we were able to repel that attack and fight another day. We spent that night clearing the wounded from the field and applying mercy to those who couldn't be helped. A steady stream of reinforcements from the army was trickling in to fill the ranks. For now, it looked like the fighting around the Wilderness would cease, and the army would move further south to put pressure on Richmond.

CHAPTER 4

*7 May 1864, 10 miles northwest
of Spotsylvania Court House.*

The fight the previous day had resulted in my promotion to Lieutenant Colonel. We received another commendation, this time from General Hancock, our Corps commander, as well as additional reinforcements on the march southeast overnight which bolstered our numbers back up to fighting strength. Our casualties for the fight in the Wilderness were sixty-seven killed, one hundred eighteen wounded, and seven missing. The whole brigade had sustained significant casualties, but was reinforced after some reorganization in the army last night.

We force marched southeast toward Spotsylvania Court House and hoped to get there before Lee. We were on Brock Road just behind Warren's V Corps, quicktime marching in line. Sedgwick's VI Corps was moving down the Orange Plank Road, as well as Burnside's IX Corps, which was opposing Richmond. Sheridan's Cavalry Corps was sent ahead to clear the road but was bogged down and had to bivouac at Todd's Tavern. General Meade, the commander of the Army of the Potomac, was infuriated and ordered them to continue. The supporting infantry had a minor scrap with a few rebs before the cavalry got there, but it was nothing monumental. The whole army was moving under the cover of darkness heading southeast with god-awful traffic blocking up the roads. The terrible conditions ruined shoes and uniforms. My hat weighed an extra pound from water weight, and the men had to give up their ponchos to cover the munitions wagons. Thousands of men and artillery trains attempting to move with haste on a narrow road for miles was a sight to see. Captain Roberts rode up to me,

"Sir."

"Captain, how may I assist you?"

"Sir, water supplies are very low. We need to replenish our canteens if we continue this force march."

"Very well. Deploy foragers."

"Yes sir."

I liked that boy. He cared more about the men than himself, and he displayed leadership qualities. The whole point of forcing this movement was to keep constant pressure on Richmond and to destroy what was left of the Army of Northern Virginia. The Army was 100,000 strong, while poor Bobby Lee only had 60,000 able-bodied men. I called them men, even though most of them were either elderly or teenagers. They were putting up a hell of a scrap though, especially on their home ground. It was bad enough fighting them in Maryland and Pennsylvania, but that was home ground, and we knew the topography of the battlefield as well as our munitions and logistical capabilities. They, however, could fortify quickly and hold a position for weeks while being outnumbered three to one. The only difference was we could replace our losses, and they couldn't. We just had to keep slaughtering them mercilessly until they surrendered. The next morning, after a long march, we would be delivering the Confederacy another heavy butcher's bill.

CHAPTER 5

*8 May 1864, Catharpin
Road, west of Todd's Tavern,
Spotsylvania Court House.*

The army was engaged all over Spotsylvania. At dawn there were cavalry skirmishes, and we were dispatched to erect defenses west of Todd's Tavern on the Catharpin Road, effectively acting as a rear-guard for the Army of the Potomac. Most of our Corps were being repulsed wherever they attacked, and were hastily constructing defenses to repel the onslaughts of rebels. Cavalry was a constant threat, and they were moving closer and closer until we finally heard their gallops from our shoddy, incomplete earthworks.

"Rise! Fix bayonets, keep a clear eye, make

sure you have loads!" I yelled as I peered through my field glasses at the foggy, muddy dirt roads surrounding us. Eventually, the dust was being kicked up in the distance, revealing a small force of cavalry with a light rebel division behind it.

"Brace yourself lads, here they come!" I shouted, as I surveyed their movements. They were testing our defenses. I turned to see General Hancock behind us, atop his horse as usual, looking disappointed that only one division was being thrown at him. They did not even bother to unlimber their artillery. They turned to approach from the north, and the lines to the far right were being engaged. Slowly, the firing continued down the line until a troop of rebel cavalry came barreling at us from straight ahead.

"Fire! Fire!" I yelled in a brief panic with a small voice crack. Their horses reared as pellets of buck and ball went screaming through their charge. After a few minutes of repulse, they retreated. What remained were a few dead and wounded horses and men. A few boys from the 32nd Connecticut and 108th New Jersey ran into the field to tend to the wounded and hopeless rebels, to provide them with some semblance of comfort.

The rest of the enemy division fell back to rejoin their main force after a few more attempts at our lines. For now at least, they fell back and were not fixing to engage us again today. General Meade was not pleased we lost the race to Spotsylvania, and was particularly critical of our cavalry and the defeat at Laurel Hill. I felt bad for Generals Sedgwick and Warren; they had not pleased the General with their performance that day.

The following day, the rebels had been busy erecting earthworks all along their lines, including Laurel Hill, which they had seized from General Warren. We were preparing to abandon our fortifications and move against the enemy. The rest of the army was entrenched opposite the rebels, with cannon and guns lined up for miles. Unfortunately, that morning, we received news that General Sedgwick had been killed from a headshot by a rebel sharp-shooter while inspecting his lines. He was beloved by his men, so I had suspected it would be a major blow to morale. Nonetheless, there were lines of battle to form and rebels to fight, so we formed our lines and began the march across the river.

Hancock knew that on their right flank the rebels had pulled back from the front of Confederate General Early's line, and he suspected the lines were moving. He had relayed this information to General Grant, who then ordered us to cross the Po River to engage the weak flank. We formed our lines of battle and began quick time marching across the river, only to halt as soon as we crossed. Soon enough, General Hancock and his staff trotted past our lines and inspected what was in front of us himself. General Hancock was concerned that our route of advance was heavily defended, and decided to halt and delay this attack until the next morning. All we could do was bivouac and wait. Men let down their equipment and rested their weary heads. I dismounted my horse and tethered him to a nearby tree, of which I laid next to him. I placed my hat over my eyes and attempted to get the best sleep I could have, knowing we would be going into action the following morning.

CHAPTER 6

10 May 1864, Across the Po River,
Spotsylvania Court House.

After some more reconnaissance we were ordered further north, leaving behind the first division under light earthworks to guard our flank. We had quickly packed up our equipment and marched into our assigned posts. Our Corps was now split, leaving us spread thin and vulnerable to attack. Overnight, Lee had been moving his lines into position to attack the isolated division to our rear. Before we knew it, and on a seemingly scheduled repetition, we heard the drums of war and bugle calls signal us to our feet to repel yet another rebel counterattack. Our isolated division was taking fire from all flanks. We force marched in battle lines at the double quick as booming artillery shook the ground around us. Elements from all of our Corps were counterattacking the rebel advances happening all over Spotsylvania. General Grant mistakenly believed the rebels had repositioned, but instead had been reinforcing their lines.

We approached the beleaguered first division and helped them get out of their ill-fated position. Rebels came pouring out of the woodwork shooting hails of gunfire at us, even charging and routing one of our regiments. They had not committed their entire force however, and they allowed us to withdraw with our battered first division.

All across the front, we were fighting tooth and nail for any advantage. We kept grinding against the rebels until they couldn't breathe and had to reposition. We kept advancing, but had not yet committed to full attack. The rest of the Army was attempting to push the rebels out of their entrenched position with little to no effect. We spent hundreds of lives only to gain a few inches of territory. But with every inch gained and every life lost, we witnessed firsthand how this war had evolved and how the new strategy would ultimately end the Confederacy. At the start of this war, we met in an open field in lines waiting to shoot each other. Now, we were inventing a new kind of warfare. Men were in trenches shooting each other just to kill one another. The cost of land kept rising and the value of the dead kept declining. We knew that we just had to keep killing the rebels to beat them. They couldn't replace their losses while we could, but we had a growing supply of widows back home. All we had to do was keep going, and the rebels would eventually wave the original Stars and Stripes over Richmond once more. As the firing ceased, the sun fell and we bivouacked after withdrawing to a safer position. We had to prepare for a very optimistic General Grant to order a full assault in the coming days.

CHAPTER 7

12 May 1864, near Brown Farm,
Spotsylvania Court House.

It was 4:30 am and we were set in position to attack the Mule Shoe. The fast and loud rain had diminished to a thick, ominous fog with a mist hovering over the wet dirt. I was standing there in my wet poncho and damp uniform, pistol and sword in hand. Laying prone behind me was the regiment ready to pounce at a moment's notice. Now with no rain, the deafening silence was filled with a discordance of bugle calls, rolling drums, and yells. I was sprinting in front of the men. It sounded like a charge of cavalry through a creek. The blockaded rebel brigade was caught unprepared and unaware as I stood atop their entrenchments shouting orders and executing young men with my pistol. Thousands of Union soldiers came pouring over the top around me, as if it were a swarm of flies, completely decimating the rebel brigade.

The 15,000 men of Hancock's Corps began overrunning the rebels at every turn. Hordes upon hordes of blue-clad soldiers were swarming the rebel trenches. Ripples of dusty blue uniforms were covering the landscape. As we moved into their entrenchments, it was discovered that the rain had ruined a large amount of their gunpowder. The disorganization began to take over the advance and men became uncontrollable. Hundreds of men began trampling each other and the rebels alike. Our breakdown in discipline and leadership had allowed the experienced Confederate leadership to reinforce their lines adequately to slow our unstoppable and chaotic advance. We had become nothing more than an armed mob. It was just like the Draft Riots of '63. We were narrowed down into a little more than a half mile front and forced to reform. The Bear Brigade was the most organized formation of the disheveled Corps. General Hancock and Gibbon were barking orders to regain order. All it was doing was buying the rebels time to reform.

General Grant had dispatched reinforcements from the V Corps and VI Corps. The fierce fighting was still unrelenting. They secured our flanks and allowed us to advance through the Mule Shoe. Brutal fighting was ongoing for hours until General Lee and General Grant simultaneously ordered attacks. We had been bogged down in the fight until thousands of rebels chanting their rebel yell came screaming at us, and simultaneously thousands of Union men charged at the same time. They met in the center of the battlefield in a titanic clash. All along the lines bayonets tore through flesh, clubs were swinging through the air, men were trampling one another. Soldiers were tackling each other and strangling each other until their necks snapped. The screams of the wounded were suppressed as their faces were being pushed into the mud and blood until they drowned in the blood, the mud, and in the tears. I was still at the head of my regiment, slashing young men with my sword. It was a brutal fight for survival. Some men had given up and were being cut through with bayonets as they threw down their arms and raised their hands in defeat. Some had fallen to their knees placing their heads in their hands wondering why they were there. Others had their heads in their hands to keep parts of their face attached.

After a while, the smell became unbearable. The insides of people were spread all over the field as if it were a new type of fertilizer. The mixture of bloated human remains, mutilated fresh corpses, and copious amounts of gunpowder had mixed an unbearable concoction. The awful sights made me sick to my stomach. There were parts of people where they shouldn't be. The visuals of grisly melee, murderous faces, and savage confusion had rocked me to my core. For one of the few moments I had to breathe, a man came up to me in tears, "Please sir, help me-". His face was all over my uniform before he could finish his sentence. The worst part of it was the sound. The explosions, gunshots, and screams of the wounded had deafened me until it was all I could hear. The screams of dying boys would haunt me for the rest of my life. I stood for a moment, shaking. I lost myself in a trance. There was absolutely nothing on my mind as I struggled to stay standing. I found myself wandering about the battlefield until somebody bumped into me, snapping me out of that spell of madness and into the real madness.

The fighting continued until the rebels decided to reposition themselves. All that was left on the field was a pavement of corpses. The front was extended all across the Mule Shoe, but the fighting came to a slow halt after a few menacing, sinister, and god-awful hours. Our casualties were capped at around nine-thousand, the rebels eight-thousand, and we took about three-thousand prisoners that day. The fight for the Mule Shoe was not over, yet the beginning of the end of the fight for all of Spotsylvania had just begun.

The next day, it was agreed at that point that the rebels were relenting, at least by our high command. The state of our Army was as well. The 69th New Jersey sustained 25% casualties that day, and the Bear Brigade approximately 45% casualties. Yet again we were at the front of the fight where we belonged. We had assumed we'd be in heavy action again, but instead the lines were reorienting. All day the rebels were repositioning their lines. We had to force march in deplorable conditions through thick rain and fog that had made the roads impassable. Still, we marched until we heard the unforgettable distant sounds of war, which was our signal to prepare for battle.

CHAPTER 8

*18 May 1864, somewhere
along the Fredericksburg Road,
Spotsylvania Court House.*

We were finally in position for the last Union assault on the Mule Shoe. Hancock's II Corps was to lead the last Union attack during the Battle of Spotsylvania Court House. We were in our battle lines for the last time on this battlefield and began marching towards the reinforced rebel position. As we approached, we came under enfilade fire and heavy artillery fire. The Bear Brigade and all of the II Corps were standing fast in the face of peril. We kept marching at them as the holes and powder burns in our regimental banners kept expanding. The optimism of high command was dropping as quickly as the men did.

We were finally close enough to fight back. Our artillery was showing them in a hail of explosions and shrapnel as we climbed over dangerous abatis. The men were firing back as best they could, but the rebel artillery fire was so devastating that their small arms fire wasn't even necessary. I was attempting to climb as best as I could alongside my men, but it was to no avail. I was shot through my shoulder as I fell back onto my men. They helped me to my feet as blood was gushing out of my open wound. All I could do was sit and watch those poor boys become impaled on the rebel defenses. Canister fire was raining down on us, just as the thick rain had the past few days. The blasts of the cannon barrels directly above us had concussed people to no end, and the canister shot was tearing them apart ruthlessly. All we were doing was sustaining casualties. There was no strategic advantage to be gained as they were perilously charged up over and over again. Soon, two whole Corps were pushing up at once in the same spot. Then another, and another. The entire Federal Army was charging up the Mule Shoe at the same time. I witnessed at least a dozen men get trampled to death in the chaos. The overwhelming force eventually made it over their perilous defenses, so the real fighting could begin.

I worked my way up to my feet and to my immediate regret, I witnessed fighting that made the action on 12th May look tame. As soon as I climbed over, wincing in pain, I was showered in the bloodied and vaporized remains of a young Confederate soldier. My pistol was drawn and I was firing frantically as hundreds of Union boys charged past me. I was leaning on the side of the rebel fortification towards the back, watching the boys of the 69th tear their way through walls of flesh with nothing but the bayonet. Captain Roberts was cut down shortly before the battle ended. He was run through with a bayonet and his insides were dispersed all over the ground.

Thousands of soldiers were intermingled and

ruthlessly brutalizing one another. The screams and chaos drove them mad. Some of them were attacking each other with severed limbs. The angry mob was growing as rebels and Federal reinforcements alike came screaming into the battle. Eventually, the fighting slowed and men fell back to their respective sides. The rebels repositioned their Army and we repositioned ours. I approached the body of Captain Roberts. The poor boy's life was cut short at the tender age of 19. I slowly closed his eyelids and fell to my knees beside him, breaking down in tears. The heavy breathing, shaking, and trembling had weakened me, not to mention my wounds. I collected myself as quickly as I could and retired from the battlefield, catching a few judgmental looks from spectators. The fight for Spotsylvania Court House slowly came to a halt and was hailed as an extremely costly victory. All we had to do was keep fighting like this, then we would win after years of pointless, devastating conflict.

CHAPTER 9

*2 June 1864, somewhere
near Old Cold Harbor, near
Mechanicsville, Virginia.*

After the technical victories at the Wilderness and Spotsylvania, both armies continued moving towards Richmond. The rebels had taken up defensive positions by the Old Cold Harbor and Petersburg. The II Corps was to move against the right flank of the Confederate Army. We had just shifted southeast from Totopotomoy Creek. The march was completely dreadful and unbearable. Upon our arrival, we were met with deplorable entrenchments. We had hundreds of cannons lining our trenches, and on the other side was Bobby Lee and his men. 35,000 men across three Union Corps were preparing to charge the tired, dirty rebels. It was the determination of General Hancock that we were, in fact, too damn tired and dirty to attack that day, and right he was. I removed my shoes when I arrived at my accommodation to find bloody stumps instead of my feet. Blood was also seeping through the bandage on my shoulder. I set up my chair, sat down, and tended to my wounds. We would be in this trench for a few days at least, so I unpacked most of my baggage. I noticed, as I was setting up my field desk, a new letter from my brother James. It read:

> *Dear Billy,*
>
> *I have just heard of the horrible and tragic events at the Wilderness and Spotsylvania. Judging by what's being printed in Harper's Weekly, I do not envy you or any of the men under your command. Unfortunately, I have terrible news. Our brother, our dear Teddy, was slain after sustaining mortal wounds in battle. He wrote to you before you departed Spotsylvania, while he was in hospital, but the letter came to me in-*

stead. He wrote how much he looked up to you and cared about you. You were in his final thoughts. I wish you luck in your future campaigns. God bless you.

Signed your dear brother,

James Johnson, United States House of Representatives.

I put down the letter as I was just beginning to shed a tear when my new second in command, Captain Jaime Murray, entered my tent.

"Sir. Men have just settled down, reporting approximately 47% casualties, sir."

"Jesus. Very well. Get yourself some rest. We're going back into action in the morning."

"Yes sir, goodnight sir."

Every day this war became more and more costly. My brother and every single casualty we took would forever remain as testaments to why we fought. It was difficult to think of my brother as a casualty or just a mere number. But I thought of the hundreds of thousands of families who had to live with that very thing because of this war. The astronomical amount of casualties we were suffering had administered a severe blow to morale, both here and at home. The bands didn't play as much as they used to, camp songs are no longer as prominent, there's less cheer, joy, laughter, and overall happiness. I don't blame them. I, too, was completely miserable. But if our sacrifices meant an end to this awful war, then I would continue doing so for years if necessary, so long as our reinforcements steadily flowed into our lines. No matter how long it would take, I would see the end to this war.

CHAPTER 10

3 June 1864, somewhere
near Old Cold Harbor, near
Mechanicsville, Virginia.

The men were roused, and so was I, in preparation for our first assault at Cold Harbor. Thousands of men were lined up in the trenches as the booms of artillery shook the ground below us.

"Square them up, Captain," I said to a nearby Captain Murray.

"Yes, sir." He began shouting, "By file into line, march!"

On the other side of the wide open field were battle-hardened rebel veterans under General John Breckenridge, the former Vice President of the United States. Our unit was filled with green troops.

Our regimental colors were flying high above our lines as were those of the entire brigade to our left and right. My uniform was covered in my blood and blood that didn't belong to me. I did my best to stitch up larger tears. The state of the Army was deplorable, but the state of the Confederacy was even worse.

Suddenly, the bugles of war sounded and the drums of war pounded. Men climbed over the top and ran across the field. Thousands of bullets were tearing through the lines as they emerged from the thick, early morning fog. I was at the front of the charge while my company commanders as well as Captain Murray were keeping the men in line. Our artillery was soaring above, creating a series of air bursting explosions above the enemy trenches. They had dozens of cannons, sending millions of pieces of shrapnel into the defenseless boys running across that field as fast as they could. We had a lot of open ground to cover. Most of the other units around us decided to fall back, but the II Corps had broken through Breckenridge's line on the left flank.

The hand-to-hand fighting had once again ensued. I had my sword and pistol drawn as I jumped into the Confederate trench. The boys were blasting rebels with buck and ball at point-blank range, completely obliterating them. It smelled of gunpowder, iron, and excrement. Bayonets were tearing through human flesh and were being driven deeper and deeper as we advanced further and further into the rebel trenches. I was cutting through men and boys, as well as emptying my pistol faster than I could be attacked.

As we were clearing out what was left of Breckenridge's command, the rebels brought their guns to bear on us. We were stuck in the narrow trench as the barrels of intimidating artillery were brought to bear on us. We captured 4 rebel guns as well as many prisoners of war, but they fired on us anyway.

"Get down boys! Stay down, get in cover!"

The ground was shaking and dirt was flying.

Explosions, dirt kicking up, fire, and endless destruction rocked us. It was not war, it was simply murder. Soon enough, the artillery slowed down and Breckenridge deployed what was left of his reserves to finish us off. Luckily, as most of the Bear Brigade was mortally wounded, Barlow's division drove them back. Us and the rest of Gibbon's division had moved to more swampy ground, which had rendered us bogged down and virtually stuck. We were cut off and encircled. All we could do was hope for a window of opportunity to escape and fall back.

CHAPTER 11

*4 June 1864, somewhere
near Old Cold Harbor, near
Mechanicsville, Virginia.*

We broke out of our encirclement and snuck back to our trenches in the dark of the night. It was a poorly coordinated assault that led to nearly 7,500 casualties. Upon your return, we found our numbers to be 149 enlisted and two officers. Captain Murray and I were the only surviving officers in the 69th New Jersey after that fateful charge. Men were being fed and rested at this point. It was determined that we would not participate in any assault until we were reinforced. Not that it mattered, anyway. Both sides were dug in to participate in true trench warfare. Sharpshooters and artillery on both sides would work tirelessly to break the other without a single conventional line formation. I retired to my accommodation to meet with Captain Murray,

"Have a seat, Captain," I said as I sat on the end of my bed.

"Sir." He took a seat on the chair at my desk.

"What do you make of all this?" I said with sincerity, "This new war."

"New war, sir?"

"This war has evolved into something else. It's not the same war as it was three years ago. What do you think of it?"

"Well, sir, I think it's the best strategy we have right now. The things we've been trying the past few years have evidently been ineffective. Maybe it's time for something new."

"Do you have any brothers, Jaime?"

"Brothers sir?" He said with a smirk, "No sir, only nine sisters. All older."

"Jesus Christ."

"Now you see why I joined the Army." We

chuckled. "How about you, sir?"

"I am the middle child of three. My older brother is in the House of Representatives, and my younger brother was just killed out west."

"I'm sorry, sir," he said as he looked down.

"How old are you, son?"

"Eighteen sir."

"A year younger than the last one."

"Last one, sir?" He said with a puzzled look on his face.

"My last executive officer. He was spilled all over the battlefield at Spotsylvania."

"I see, sir." There was an awkward pause."Is there anything else you need, sir?"

"No, thank you. You are dismissed."

"Sir." He exited the tent.

There was something unique about that boy. He seemed to have a way about himself. I sat at my desk and composed a letter to my brother:

Dear James,

I have just received the news you have disclosed to me. My heart is broken for Mother. We have claimed victories at the Wilderness and Spotsylvania and now are entrenched at Old Cold Harbor. The spirits of the men are low. We had attacked yesterday, but that ended in disaster. We are now engaged in a stalemate and stuck in our respective trenches. Give Mother my best.

Signed your dear brother,

Lieutenant Colonel William Johnson, Commanding Officer, 69th New Jersey Volunteer Infantry.

"Dispatch!" I shouted as he was passing by collecting letters.

I handed him the letter and retired into my tent. God knows how long we would be stuck in these terrible trenches. I was growing miserable of them already, and we had just got there.

CHAPTER 12

10 June 1864, somewhere
near Old Cold Harbor, near
Mechanicsville, Virginia.

Now that we were finally in temporary quarters with more than cold wet dirt to sleep in, I was awoken every hour on the hour, afflicted with awful night terrors for the past six nights. I fell asleep every night to the sounds of sharpshooters, yet all I heard when I closed my eyes were the screams of the wounded. Drenched in a cold sweat, I dreamed that my brother's lifeless corpse was on the ground next to me. When I leant over to check on him, he sat up with the speed of a racehorse, and placed his hand forcefully on my throat. He looked me deep in my eyes, showing me the corpse of every man killed under my command. I woke up seconds after that. The rest of those tireless nights were spent endlessly pacing my tent. I spent hours and hours staring into a cold and empty abyss until it was time to go back to bed. Every morning, Captain Murray brought me coffee and some form of food, which I fortunately and gratefully ate. After I finished, I went straight back to nothing. For the life of me, I could not figure out what the problem was. I was never like this before the war. I suppose war changes people in ways they could never predict. The only thing truly keeping me sane was the insanity of battle. The times we spent off the field truly took their toll on me. Before long, I began to indulge in an old hobby. A swig from a hidden flask eased the nerves. The drink made me feel as if my mind were completely at ease. I stumbled around my tent in a ragged old nightgown until I passed out. I woke up the next morning with a pounding headache and regret.

When wandering about the trenches, you weren't allowed to stand up straight, for fear of rebel sharpshooters. The occasional artillery shell made most people stay where they were, and the many unlucky who fell to sharpshooters or artillery were removed from the trench after a while. Mail was still going in and out every day, and food was somewhat abundant. Life in the trenches wasn't exactly pleasant by any means. While we had some more safety than a battlefield tent, the trenches were incredibly cramped. Not to mention the stench. I was one of the lucky few officers who got accommodation for themselves. In some places along the extensive lines, we were only yards apart from the opposing lines. The people who had it the worst were the people in between the lines. The people wounded enough to be immobile, but not wounded enough to die. They had to lay there, with no assistance. There were thousands of people screaming for any help whether it be food, water, or medical attention. Nobody could help them without falling victim to those vultures. And to top it all off, after days of casualty counts, it was discovered that our brigade commander, Colonel Morely, was killed in that last assault. His remains were discovered by our picket line in two separate sections of our lines.

News spread quickly of the Colonel's death, when finally I received a letter from General Gibbon, our division commander:

Lieutenant Colonel William Johnson,

I've received word of the death of Colonel Morely. I've also heard of the death of your brother. There is little more pain one man can feel than the loss of a brother. I offer my most sincere condolences. The command of the fifth brigade is vacant and in need of replacement, and there are few people I trust with this responsibility. I have faith in you. Command has already approved of your promotion. Congratulations, Colonel.

Signed, Brigadier General John Gibbon, Commanding Officer 2nd Division, II Corps.

I held that letter in my hand for an hour. I was

petrified of the new responsibility. I presided over an entire brigade of Federal troops. We were a veteran force, and I knew and trusted all of the regimental commanders, but the prospect seemed daunting. I called Captain Murray into my tent.

He sprinted in, out of breath. "Sir."

"I've just been promoted to colonel of the brigade. I'm bumping you up to major and putting you in charge of the 69th. Congratulations."

"Thank you, sir. Congratulations," he said with a proud, accomplished look on his face.

"Don't get too excited, I didn't get you approved yet. I'll compose a letter for you to take to command."

"Yes sir. Thank you, sir."

We sat in an awkward silence as I composed a short letter.

"Here, send this off."

"Thank you, sir."

He sped off with a smile on his face. I stepped out of my tent for a breath of fresh air as I watched him walk down the line. He was standing up straight and walking rather slowly. Suddenly, a shot rang out and the whiz of the bullet threw me to the ground in reflex. When I looked, I saw Major Murray laying on the ground, completely still. I walked over to check on him as he stood up slowly with his hat in his hand. I kneeled next to him in fear. He held his hat up to find a bullet hole in the brim. We laughed as he slowly stood up and walked to command, as I sighed in relief.

The Battle of Cold Harbor had ended in Union defeat. We suffered as many casualties in the trenches as we did in the major assaults. The new trench warfare was brutal, slow, and deplorable. The Overland Campaign was a major success, however. We achieved our goal in forcing the rebels back near Richmond and launching unrelenting attacks, so they couldn't replace their losses. We kept fighting them so they couldn't breathe, and we finally forced them to within range of their capital. We still had a war to fight and I was not sure where we would be

going next, but I knew the Confederacy was waver-
ing.

PART 2: THE RICHMOND-PETERSBURG CAMPAIGN

◆ ◆ ◆

LIEUTENANT GENERAL ULYSSES S. GRANT'S UNION ARMY

◆ ◆ ◆

Major General Meade's Army
of the Potomac,
Major General Hancock's II Corps,
Second Division, Fifth Brigade,
Colonel Bill Johnson, Commanding.

CHAPTER 13

*15 June 1864, Somewhere
near Petersburg, Virginia.*

The Union Army of the Potomac and the Army of the James were marching towards the critical railroad junction and commercial hub of Petersburg, Virginia. The south was desperately scraping for any conscripts to slow or halt the inevitable Union onslaught. There were fewer than 15,000 of those conscripts under General Beauregard to defend against 50,000 fresh Union troops. Detachments from the Army of the James had been assaulting the Dimmock Line of the Petersburg defenses over the past week, while the Army of the Potomac was now slowly making its way into the vicinity of the battlefield. Each of the four infantry Corps were slowly trickling into the Petersburg trenches, preparing to assault the rebel positions. General Hancock was in temporary command of the Army of the Potomac while General Meade was still en route, and we were nearly there.

The fifth "Bear" brigade was chock-full of fresh troops and veterans alike. Each of the six regimental commanders were fresh commanders, as the previous veteran commanders were mortally wounded or killed in the last campaign. Major Murray was the best of the six, in command of my former regiment, the 69th New Jersey Volunteer Infantry. They had all received new regimental banners with the names of the battles participated in during the Overland Campaign stitched onto their flags. The Brigade had been the same since each of the respective regiments were mustered in October of 1862. We had always been the fifth brigade of the II Corps. There were approximately two dozen veterans who had been in service of the fifth brigade since our first steps onto the battlefield at Fredericksburg, myself being one of them. Half of the replacements were veterans from other regiments that were assimilated and were in the II Corps and the other half were new volunteers or draftees, courtesy of President Lincoln.

I had been having manic episodes as well as spells of depression ever since I took command of the brigade. My vision became blurred, my thoughts became tainted with the screams and cries of the dead. For hours at a time I would scream, crawl, cry, and beg. When we left Cold Harbor, I lost access to my liquor and the manic episodes became even more severe. My fear of insanity was becoming a reality. I no longer became disturbed by brain matter and blood spraying on my uniform. The reality of war became normal to me after years of brutal atrocities. I will never forget the first time I saw the true reality of war. In 1862, when we charged the stonewall at Fredericksburg, I had dropped my rifle to pick up the fallen banner of the 69th. When I lifted the flag, the original flag bearers' insides were splayed out and had covered the flag that I was now carrying. I became sick to my stomach and vomited as I carried the flag into battle. Now, in 1864, the sights, smells, sounds, and the feeling of war became home. The contrast between then and now was astonishing.

Soldiers from the Army of the James as well as a few advance detachments from the Army of the Potomac were relentlessly assaulting the rebel positions still, even as we were arriving. Now that the bulk of the army was arriving, we could begin full-scale assaults on the rebels and hopefully drive them out of their defenses over the next few days. Unfortunately, we were arriving as the rebels stripped several of their defensive lines to reinforce the ones we were digging in to assault. The useless Generals in high command had failed to capitalize on this opportunity to interpose between Lee and Richmond. This was going to be an even more brutal and costly offensive.

CHAPTER 14

16 June 1864, Petersburg, Virginia.

◆ ◆ ◆

There were more than 14,000 rebels in their defensive line. General Beauregard had committed his last reserves in a ditch attempt to hold the last bastion of defense before Richmond. 50,000 Union soldiers stared down his meager defenses and prepared for a full assault. The II Corps would lead the first major assault on the Confederate defenses at Petersburg. General Gibbon's second division would be the spearhead of the attack, with the fifth brigade at the very front. The "Bear" brigade was lining up in offensive columns as I heard regimental commanders shouting orders as I passed by,

"69th! By file into line, march!" Shouted Major

Murray at the battle ready 69th New Jersey.

"Double ranks Major. Bayonets and Buck and Ball." I said sternly as I adjusted my gloves.

"Yes sir." He turned to give the orders.

All three Corps slowly moved forward and we were marching at the front. We were to be the first faces the enemy saw that day. I was at the front of the Brigade, walking several yards ahead of them all by my lonesome. There was a small defilade they halted in.

"Stay here, I'll give the signal," I whispered to a nearby officer.

I slowly walked to the crest of the hill. I emerged to see trenches lined with rebels, and behind that were batteries of artillery with crews ready to fire. I kept walking until I was standing straight up in the middle of the battlefield by my-self. I raised my field glasses and looked at a General sitting atop his horse behind the rebel artillery. I looked at him and he looked at me. We were locked in a stare as he lowered his glasses, revealing the face of General Beauregard. He began shouting in the distance and men were scrambling.

"Charge!" I shouted as I waved my sword in a rally for advance.

The "Bear" brigade ran over the hill and a wave of blue clad uniforms began barreling towards the defenders. Soon the booms of artillery began and shots started sailing overhead, exploding, and causing ruptures to appear in the lines. Canister shot was cutting through the men at unfathomable rates. The men were running frantically and had started to get close enough for small arms fire. Thousands of bullets came screaming through the air, bringing men to their knees then face down on the dirt as they were running. If someone was wounded at the front of the charge, they would likely die during the charge as they would get trampled to death. Some company commanders halted and formed a line to volley, while others simply kept running. The familiarity of the battlefield brought me comfort and clarity. I finally reached the top of their trench, with the brigade close behind me. It was filled with mud and blood, there were very few defenders left. I entered the trench with my pistol drawn and aimed at a nearby corner. Other Union soldiers were clearing the rest of the trenches as the charge had achieved its objective. I slowly approached the corner and quickly turned to find a cowering 11-year-old boy holding a rifle twice the size of him incorrectly and crying against the wall. I damn near shot him as he fell to the ground whimpering in fear. I quickly holstered my pistol and ordered the men to clear the rest of the trenches.

"Get out of here, make sure it's clear," I yelled to a nearby squad.

"Yes, sir." They quickly scurried in the opposite direction.

"It's ok, boy." I calmly said to him as I removed my coat and placed it on the boy as a blanket. He was a scrawny, blonde haired, blue-eyed kid who had no business on a battlefield,

"What's your name, boy?" I said as I kneeled

in front of him.

"J- Joshua." He said with a deep southern accent as he averted his eyes with tears streaming down his face.

"It's ok, Joshua," I said as a mysterious noise grew louder and louder. "Stay here."

I stood up to look over the top of the trenches on the opposite side. It was the cursed rebel yell. There were thousands of rebel reinforcements with their regimental banners waving high, running at us.

"Stay down, Joshua." He covered his head and hid in the corner.

"Here they come! Prepare to defend yourselves!" I yelled to the men in the trenches.

Men lined the sides of the trenches to repel the counterattack. The only unit in the trenches was the second division. The rest were defending redoubts which they had just successfully seized and were surrounding us. Hundreds of guns began firing devastating buck and ball shot at the onslaught of rebels. Hundreds of them were falling, but they had not relented and were still coming. They kept getting closer and looked as if they outnumbered us three to one. I holstered my weapons, picked up Joshua and ran back to our defensive positions. I was running across the field with this kid in my arms, almost as if I had no control over what I was doing. Thankfully, as I approached our lines, the guards were distracted and I was able to get into my tent with Joshua without anyone noticing. I placed him on my bed,

"Stay here, I'll be right back," I said, out of breath, as I immediately ran out the front.

I stood outside my tent and watched as the rebel flags re-entered their trenches and Union flags approached our trenches. Our charge was successful and we took our objective, but their counterattack was too, and they were able to retake the objective. The survivors ran back to our trenches, tired, bloody, and dirty, and finally got some much-needed rest. I walked back into my tent and saw Joshua asleep on my bed, at peace. I set up my chair and slept in it for the night. The boy needed the rest.

CHAPTER 15

17 June 1864, Petersburg, Virginia.

I woke up the next morning with a pounding headache and blurred vision. When I finally came to my senses, I saw Joshua was about to walk out of the tent,

"Woah, woah, boy. You can't just wander out there." I said as I jumped up, grabbed his arm, and sat him in the chair.

"Why not?" he said with genuine curiosity.

"Because," I paused, "you aren't supposed to be here." We locked eye contact. He began to cry.

"It's alright." I kneeled next to him. "I'll take care of you until we get you back to your family." I gave him a quick hug.

"But- th- they're all dead. You people killed

them." He locked eyes with me again.

"Look- I'm sorry." We sat in silence for a little bit.

"Are you hungry? When was the last time you ate?" I asked.

"I haven't," he responded as he wiped his soot-covered face.

"Here, eat this." I handed him some hard tack.

"Thank you." He gnawed on it.

"I will be busy for a bit. There are a few books in that bag. Stay here until I get back." I said as I donned my blood-stained uniform and walked out the front into the air filled with booming artillery and toxic smoke. The trenches stretched for miles and consisted of dozens of redoubts on both sides. Artillery and infantry lined both trench systems and incessantly fired at one another, which would render visibility a luxury. The trenches here were cramped, dirty, dusty, and completely deplorable. Most people didn't have space for themselves. Only officers Colonel and above were allowed to have personal accommodations. The rest were subject to the hellish and inhuman pig sty.

General Grant had arrived with Burnside's IX Corps and was tending to battlefield command. General Hancock was still in command of the Army of the Potomac, as General Meade had still not yet arrived. They had launched a surprise attack at dawn and seized several rebel positions as well as hundreds of prisoners. As they tried to move, they became entangled by logs and ravines which subjected them to enfilade fire which stifled their advance. Beauregard was trying to construct new defenses west of the Dimmock line, but was crippled by an extreme lack of manpower. The IX Corps had launched another attack midday, but was again subjected to enfilade fire and could not advance.

I made my way back to the tent as the mail was about to be dropped off. I quickly grabbed my parcels from the soldier and entered the tent, dismissing him. I sorted through my mail and opened a letter from James.

Dear Billy,

After a series of wise investments, I am pleased to inform you that the railroad company's profits have increased tenfold. The business is thriving with the expansion westward, and the government is in desperate need of steel. I have purchased majority shares in major steel companies throughout the northeast and made us the majority shareholder. We now have government contracts to construct rail out west. I have spoken directly to President Lincoln regarding the railroad contracts, and he mentioned you. He is thankful for your service, and sorry for our loss.

Signed your dear brother,

James Johnson, United States House of Representatives.

The news was incredible. Our family would no longer have the issue of money. I was looking forward to a time of peace and prosperity after the war. The unbearable weight was finally off our shoulders, particularly mothers. Most of the people in our area of the state were failed businessmen. The only income they had were their small farms. Those farms had unfortunately relied on slave labor. Granted, there were only a few slaves on each farm, nothing compared to the south, but it was an interesting prospect to consider. A northern state with thousands of volunteers fighting against the very thing that many people in the state rely on. It was also somewhat symbolic. I then began to think of people like poor Joshua. He had nothing, he lost everything he once had. I looked up to find Joshua sitting at my desk struggling to read as I readied for bed.

"You can't stay here forever, you know. We're going to have to do something with you."

"I want to go home." He said without looking up from his book, straining his eyes.

"I know, but you can't just yet. I'm going to take care of you until I can get you home, safely," I said as I lay down in my bed.

"Yeah..."

I felt horrible for the kid. He lost his family and was forced to fight in a war he had nothing to do with. The poor kid could barely read. Just as I was about to fall asleep, I took a swig from my flask. I found that I was not enjoying the liquor as much as I was before. It left a sour taste in my mouth and a horrible feeling in my mind. Nonetheless, I shut my eyes for the first time in a long time for some much-needed sleep.

CHAPTER 16

18 June 1864, Petersburg, Virginia.

When we woke up, we found the rebel lines to be reinforced and battle-ready. Beauregard had 20,000 men waiting for a Union charge. Fortunately, the Union lines were augmented and reinforced as well, numbered 67,000. I suspected it wouldn't make a difference, however. It didn't matter how many people were on the ground, so long as the ground was good and the thing they were standing behind could stop a bullet. The rebels were extra dug in with reinforced, resupplied, and fresh batteries of artillery and brigades of infantry. To make things even worse, General Hancock had to be relieved due to lingering effects from an old wound he sustained at the Battle of Gettysburg. He was replaced by General Birney. We were as ready as we could've been, the sooner we attacked, the better the chance we had of dislodging the Confederates from their position. I walked over to Joshua, who was having his breakfast.

"We're going out again today. Stay here, I'll be back," I said, holstering my Colt.

"Alright. I'll be here," he said with a disappointed tone.

I walked out of the tent to see the men of the II Corps forming battle lines. The 20th Vermont Infantry regiment of the fifth "Bear" brigade was forming triple ranks, a massive target for artillery.

"Major! This is unacceptable," I told the commander, "Do you genuinely believe that triple ranks won't be a target for artillery?!" He stammered as I cut him off.

"If you form triple ranks, you won't have any ranks left! Reform them, damn you!" I was screaming at the top of my lungs. The confused commander looked at me.

"Sir?" the puzzled 18-year-old boy looked at me.

"Mend your lines, Major!"

"Yes, sir!" He responded as he quickly fixed his posture and began issuing orders.

Now with proper battle lines, the brigade was ready to embark on an assault on the rebel trenches. The men had started marching over the top of the trenches. We were making steady progress and meeting pitiful resistance. Barely any casualties were taken, as sparse artillery fire and gunshots rendered meager results. We advanced all the way forward into the first rebel trenches, capturing them with no resistance. Suddenly, we looked beyond the trenches to see fresh batteries of artillery, and the line of rebel infantry in their new defensive positions.

"Brace boys! Get ready to charge!" I shouted, as men lined up on the walls of the trenches next to me, preparing for a storm of iron and lead. Some of the men even turned the rebel guns against them.

The sharpshooters had started doing their work as well.

The booms of artillery immediately filled the air alongside smoke, shrapnel, explosions, and bullets as the men climbed over the top again as we advanced towards the rebel's defensive positions. Our advance ground to a halt as we became bogged down by poor terrain and deplorable visibility. We fought for a long time, taking significant casualties, before the IX and V Corps came up to reinforce us. I was with the Bear brigade, laying prone alongside them, as they fired independently as they saw targets. Men of the rest of the army had attempted to attack the rebel lines, but would meet the same problems as us. They became bogged down and ground to a halt in the marshes and thick smoke. Before long, the V Corps attempted a daring assault. They marched in front of us, not several yards in front of us, and prepared for an advance. Colonel Joshua Chamberlain leading the assault had even greeted me as they passed by. They advanced towards the

Dimmock line, led by the famous Colonel, and were halted by Rive's Salient. Murderous firepower rained down on them, bringing their ambitious assault to a firm halt and rendering Colonel Chamberlain severely wounded.

We were getting desperate. We longed for any break in the rebel line. General Meade had organized a last daring attack for the entire army. Regimental banners rippled in the gust of wind that was behind us as we stood up. The dusk light was in front of us, and so were the rebels. We stood in our battle lines and awaited the assault to begin. Before long, the drums of war sounded and men began to attack. Dozens of rebel guns and thousands of rebel rifles began showering us in immeasurable amounts of lethal metal. I was personally leading the brigade as they ground up against the rebel fortifications. All four Corps of the Army of the Potomac were advancing against this impossible rebel position. It was an overwhelming moment as my head began to spin yet again. My vision became blurred. I collapsed on the battlefield for an unknown amount of time. As I came to, I was directly in front of the rebel trench, with most of the army in retreat back to the friendly trenches. The sun was nearly down as the silhouette of a rebel rifle pointed at me. I met the rifle with my own pistol and fired as he fired. My shot killed him, and his shot entered my side. His body fell down on top of me as I was writhing in pain on the ground.

I checked the wound and determined it was merely superficial, and my primary concern was to get back to the friendly lines. The route back was paved with the wounded, dead, and dying. As I hobbled back, I found a wounded soldier asking for help. He had such an innocent look in his eye. To my right, there was another. In front of me and to the rear of me there were more. All of them were begging me for help. I had a distance to cover and did not want to waste time. Behind one of them was a large regimental banner. I walked over to it and laid it flat on the ground. I dragged as many of the wounded onto it as I could manage and rolled the pole inward to use it as a handle. Coincidentally, and rather dramatically, it was the regimental banner of the 69th New Jersey Infantry. I dragged them behind me, using every ounce of my body to bring them back, while my wound was bleeding and my mind was fogged. Fortunately, before I lost consciousness again, we made it back to the friendly lines. The wounded were taken care of, and I was patched up by a regimental surgeon. I limped back to my tent, barely conscious, as men applauded my return and congratulated me for saving those men. A few of them called me a hero. I stopped in my tracks.

"I am not a hero. The men who aren't walking in this trench and are instead laying dead on another battlefield of this damned war are the heroes," I said as I climbed atop a barricade to deliver a speech. "The heroes of this war are not to have died in vain. For too long, we have been on the many battlefields of this war. For too long, children have been slaughtered for nothing. For too damn long, we've had to prove time and time again that the blessings of liberty shall be preserved always and forever. For too long, we've had to flaunt our resolve and willingness to defend what's right. I, for one, will never stop so long as there is breath in my lungs, blood in my veins, thoughts in my head, and sweat on my brow. I don't care what your color, race, creed, opinions, religion, preferences, or any number of differences are. So long as the people stand united against one common enemy, the United States will live always and forever. Lest we forget the fallen heroes, remember them for what they have done for us, not what they could have done." I stepped down from the barricade. I looked to my left and saw General Grant himself standing there, staring at me. He hadn't broken eye contact, and started applauding. Soon the whole army began cheering. I entered my tent through a jubilant crowd and immediately fell asleep on my cot, face down, completely by-passing Joshua who had fallen asleep at my chair.

The Second Battle of Petersburg had ended with no results in four days of ruthless assaults.

Union casualties exceeded 12,000 and Confederate casualties had exceeded 5,000. And no ground was taken from the rebels. General Meade had now ordered the army to dig in and prepare for a long and arduous siege.

CHAPTER 17

20 June 1864, Petersburg, Virginia.

I had known Joshua for a grand total of four days, and already we were becoming fond of each other. He seemed to be relying on me for guidance and yearned to be educated. I found myself relying on him for some sense of comfort. He brought me away from the war in my mind, and gave me a purpose. I was teaching him how to read, feeding him, and attempting to care for him in any way he needed. He was still shy and reserved, which was to be expected, but I felt it was a necessary change of pace from the battlefield.

The fifth brigade had suffered nearly irreparable losses during the four days of assaults leading up, so we were kept in the trenches for garrison duty while the rest of the II Corps marched on the rebels in the surrounding area. We would be here for a while as reinforcements and supplies would be prioritized for units attempting to break the siege. Besides the constant sharpshooter problem and the occasional artillery shell, life in the trenches was slow and boring. The mail was still running as I had sent off another letter to my brother.

Dearest James,

I am ecstatic to hear the news of the railroad investments. The army is now besieging the commercial hub of Petersburg, Virginia. I have been wounded several times since the start of the Overland Campaign but am now nearly recovered. We had suffered agonizing losses during the initial assaults and are now limited to garrison duty in the trenches until our numbers get back up to fighting strength. I can assure you my safety for the time being. Also, a small boy by the name of Joshua is now under my care. He was picked up in one of the assaults before we were pushed back.

Signed, Colonel William Johnson, commanding officer, fifth brigade, second division, II Corps.

I entered the tent to find Joshua sitting at my desk,

"Billy, how do you say this word?" He gestured towards the word *independence,*

"In-de-pen-dence," I said as I pointed out each syllable, reading it together with him.

"How did you know my name was Billy? I don't think I ever told you that," I said with a puzzled, yet intrigued expression.

"I read one of your letters. Sorry about your brother," he said with utmost sincerity. I looked at him as if to reprimand him, but he was just a boy, learning and listening to what I was saying. It was a nice feeling.

"Thank you. You shouldn't be reading any letters, though. You can read all the books you like," I said as I filed away the rest of my letters.

He looked down at the book. "I'm sorry."

"It's alright, buddy." I began to work on a daily report.

The surrounding army was looking for creative ways to break the rebel defenses. Elements of the II, XI, V, and VI Corps were dispatched to disrupt logistics, cut telegraph wire, and destroy miles of railroad leading into Petersburg. The plan was to starve them out, beat them down, and pave the way to Richmond. Well-off political generals were even purchasing the very new and extremely expensive Gatling guns to place along the trenches. We had about eight of them spread throughout the trench system. Each of them had to be manned by a battery crew. They were amazing new machines. They could fire 200 rounds per minute, more than most lines of infantry, and had up to ten barrels each. Every now and again, we'd hear them fire, and it sounded as if several companies of infantry were ripple firing down a line a hundred yards long. They could be extremely effective in a line battle, but from what I've seen in these trenches, they are mostly ineffective. It was still interesting to be living in a time of such drastic warfare evolution. Two years prior, we were charging a stonewall at Fredericksburg, and dying in a field, with no cover. Now, we were fighting in trenches with this new technology and new methods of warfare. Such drastic warfare innovation and evolution had not been seen at this scale since the era of Napoleon.

CHAPTER 18

22 June 1864, Petersburg, Virginia.

A new course of action had dawned on the horizon. It was evident that a new era of technology and warfare had spawned out of three bloody years of war. Nobody was going to break through on either side using conventional methods. Any effort was wasted trying to assault the trenches directly. The people there, including me, would learn to live with constant musketry and artillery booming. Joshua would sleep with wads of paper in his ears every night to drown out the sound. I would try to force liquor down my gullet, it was painful, but the only way I could sleep. I learned to live with the constant headache. I wasn't sure if the headache was from the constant paperwork or copious amount of liquor that I had been pounding, but I was living with it.

Every so often, I would notice the strong scent of cigars, which signified the legendary General Grant passing by. I hated tobacco, then again, General Grant abhorred the drink and adored tobacco while I was the direct opposite. I truly hated both, but I couldn't stop myself from liquor. I passed most of my time boorishly signing reports and sleeping, while Joshua mostly read books, both of us barely leaving the confines of the tent. I then sorted through the mail to find another letter from James.

Dearest Billy,

Your safety is a welcome piece of news. It is good to hear of your new company. I do hope he can be safely returned home after this awful war. The railroad investments have been paying back monumentally, your share has been doubling and tripling. I do hope that the promise of your safety remains fulfilled, Mother has been worried sick.   *Signed your dear brother,*

James Johnson, United States House of Represen-

tatives

As I was putting the letter away, I heard a knock at the entrance.

"Colonel Johnson?" the calm, mild, and vaguely familiar voice spoke.

"Yes." I said, noticing the strong scent of tobacco. I slowly looked up to see the legendary General Grant standing before me.

"Sir." I stood at attention and saluted,

"At ease. I have heard tell of a young boy under your care. I see the rumors are true." General Grant and his entourage eyed Joshua and the empty bottles around the table.

"What's your name, son?" he asked with a light smile.

"Joshua." He looked as if he had the fear of God in him. General Grant turned to face me.

"Colonel, you have committed yourself entirely to this army and rendered your service invaluable. I credit you with many battlefield victories, bravery in the field, and various acts of heroism. This is an unusual situation. Children are in no circumstances allowed in the vicinity of this battlefield," he said in a calm tone.

"Yes sir, but this boy cannot be left alone. He has no one to care for him-". I was cut off.

"Which is why I am allowing him to remain under your care for the time being. Now, there is a major operation coming up of which I will need use of your brigade to bolster the Ninth Corps. You will receive correspondence regarding that in the coming weeks. General Burnside looks forward to working with you. In addition, you are being promoted to brevet Brigadier General," he handed me the papers, "courtesy of President Lincoln." He exited the tent, leaving a puff of cigar smoke in his wake.

CHAPTER 19

1 July 1864, Petersburg, Virginia.

After a week of cleaning up my act, I had expelled all remaining liquor from my possession. I had been staying up late at night to assist Joshua with his reading, and had been regularly inspecting the brigade with my new shoulder boards indicating Brigadier General. I had shaved my long, unkept beard and styled my mustache. I was sporting a thick and fine goatee as well as a hardy hat with a large feather and a pristine new uniform with a sword customized with a gilded hilt. I walked with confidence, an heir of wisdom, and was ready for whatever was to be thrown at me. The brigade was as ready as ever with fresh reinforcements numbering around one-thousand with new officers and new regimental banners. They spent hour after hour training for the past five days and preparing for orders to move. To my side was Joshua with a fresh set of clothes and new books. He was something of an aide-de-camp to me now. He boosted morale, being he was just a little kid, two feet shorter than me. My brigade staff consisted of myself; Major Steven Stillwell, the new adjutant; Dr. Matthew Jackson, the new brigade surgeon; Captain Andrew Lowell, the new brigade quartermaster; Lieutenants Mark Baird and Richard Montgomery, the aides-de-camp; and finally Lieutenant Joe Baxter, the commissary officer. All of these men traveled with me in addition to little Joshua.

With this new staff, fresh troops, and new uniforms, we finally had new orders in hand. Major Stillwell handed me the orders.

"From General Burnside," He said as I opened the letter.

General Johnson,

You and your brigade are to report to the IX Corps sector and assist in mine construction. Our objective is to construct a tunnel beneath the Confederate Lines and detonate several tons of gunpowder below them, obliterating a hole in their lines. After your brigade assists in construction and transport of the powder, you will assist in the assault on the broken lines. Once your brigade reaches the IX Corps sector, meet me in my headquarters.

Signed, Major General Ambrose Burnside, Commanding Officer, IX Army Corps.

"Well, gentlemen, move the brigade to the IX Corps sector," I said as I folded the letter in my hands.

"Yes sir," replied the entourage of officers as they began to shout orders.

The entire brigade began moving to the IX Corps sector. It would take a day or two to move everything through the trenches. I began to pack up my quarters, and moved with the brigade to our new post.

CHAPTER 20

2 July 1864, Petersburg, Virginia.

As we settled into our semi-permanent station, I prepared to meet with Major General Ambrose Burnside. He was known as an honest, unimaginative, social type. However, he was the one who, at the time as the Commander of the Army of the Potomac, had overseen the slaughter of thousands of men at the stonewall during the Battle of Fredericksburg, when I was a young officer. He was solely responsible for that demoralizing defeat. Now, I had to meet him and remain under his command for one of the riskiest ideas in human history. Construct a mine beneath the Confederate entrenchments and detonate 8,000 pounds of gunpowder beneath them, then assault the hole in their line. I had never heard of such a ridiculous plan before, but my respect for military tradition and the chain of command had overruled my personal opinions on this would-be failure.

I approached the headquarters of General Burnside and entered to see General Burnside standing alongside an unknown Lieutenant Colonel, General Meade, and the various division commanders of the IX Corps.

"General Burnside. I'm General William Johnson, Commander of the fifth brigade, second division, second Corps. I've been dispatched to assist you with your plan, sir," I said as I removed my hat and awaited a response. The tension in the air could be cut with a knife.

"General! Excellent to see you. This is Lieutenant Colonel Pleasants, the mastermind behind the plan. This is General Meade, as you know. Over here we have General Ledlie, First Division Commander; General Potter, Second Division,;General Willcox, Third Division; and finally, General Ferrero, Fourth

Division." He handed me a glass of wine. The inside of his headquarters was reminiscent of the finest hotel. There were crystal decanters in every corner, a small chandelier above the table we were standing around, a map was draped over the most fine silk tablecloth, and the finest pieces of furniture. With every boom of a distant cannon, there was a slight jingle from the crystal chandelier that only made the sparkle more impressive.

"Excellent to meet you, gentlemen." We all shook hands and exchanged pleasantries.

"Well, General, how can I assist you?" I asked as the room fell silent.

"I remain under the assumption that you understand the premise of the plan?" General Burnside said with a flare in his eyes.

"Yes sir. What can the Bear Brigade do for you?" I inquired.

"Bear Brigade?" he asked curiously.

"An affectionate nickname afforded by the men," General Meade turned to General Burnside.

"One of the best brigades in the army. Damn near legendary." The General raised his glass at me, I raised mine.

"Glad to hear I have the right group for the job. General, all I need from you is your cooperation. If your men don't mind moving dirt and gunpowder around alongside Colonel Pleasants Pennsylvanian miners, then we can do business," he said as he sipped his wine.

"That can be arranged." I sipped mine.

"Good. Now, after the hole is blown, all I need you to do from there is follow the lead of the coloreds under General Ferrero. They are being specifically trained for this job-". General Meade cut off General Burnside.

"I'm not so sure about using the coloreds for this one, Ambrose. Northern newspapers would eat up a slaughter of that nature," he said with an heir of caution. General Burnside protested.

"I've already dispatched the orders, General. I have complete faith that they will be able to handle this," said the agitated General. General Meade fell silent.

"As I was saying, you will follow their lead. A brigade will go right, and a brigade will go left, and you will follow after seeing which side requires more assistance. You will act as something of a veteran auxiliary reserve. Understood General?" he said.

"Yes sir." I put down my empty glass.

"Now gentlemen, that is all we have to discuss for tonight. Let's end the war this month. I wish you all a restful night," announced General Burnside.

All the men exchanged goodbyes and I left for my bed, which I long desired. The interior of my headquarters was reminiscent of the most bland frontier cabin. I had a field desk, my own cot, wooden chairs, candles, a mirror complete with a basin, and a small wardrobe. I quickly wrote the orders to my staff on my modest desk and dispatched the orders. I said goodnight to Joshua, who now had his own cot, and fell asleep for the night, not desiring to embark on this treacherous assault in the coming weeks.

CHAPTER 21

4 July 1864, Petersburg, Virginia.

Now, with the men assisting the IX Corps in their mine construction and gunpowder transportation, all we had to do was wait for the completion and detonation. It was the fourth of July and the men were enjoying extra rations and celebrating the 88th anniversary of our nation's independence. I was only indulging in some wine and fresh fruit, as was Joshua. It was an incredible day with reason to celebrate. Suddenly, a man entered my tent, placed a letter on my desk, and walked out quickly. I stood up and examined the letter. It was from Washington D.C. It read:

Brigadier General William Johnson,

I regret to inform you that your brother, James, was killed on July 1st by a Confederate Sharpshooter while riding in a carriage just outside Washington. It is with utmost sincerity and solemnity that I inform you of my condolences. I understand this is the second of two brothers that you have lost in this awful conflict. I have taken special care to ensure that they are both buried at a place of your choosing. I wish to meet you after the war and offer you my most sincere condolences in person. General Grant has spoken highly of you and earned you a place in my heart with the tales he has regaled of your services. Godspeed to you, sir.

Signed, A. Lincoln, President of the United States.

I had a feeling the lack of correspondence from my brother was no coincidence. Tears fell from my eyes as I placed the letter down and put my head in my hands. Everything had been going so well, it was expected that there would be unwelcome news. I could not believe that he was assassinated by a rebel that close to the capitol. It was as if the fighting we were doing out here had no bearing on the safety of our families at home. It inspired me to give no quarter to any rebel we met on the battlefield. I summoned my staff.

"Gentlemen, due to some personal issues, I should like to remain unbothered for the next 24 hours. Unless the rebels miraculously storm our trenches, I'll see you all tomorrow. I'd like to have a staff meeting sometime next week or the week after." I laid back in my cot.

"Very well, sir. Summon us should you need us," replied Major Stillwell.

"Thank you, gentlemen. Enjoy the festivities." They exited the tent.

I sat in my cot for hours as the day turned to night. Fireworks lit up the night sky as it became difficult to discern the boom of a firework from that of artillery. All of my childhood memories flashed before my eyes. I remembered the last time my brothers and I were all in the same place together. On April 16th, 1861, James, Teddy, and I were all standing on the street reading the same newspaper that I was holding. It was news of the attack on Fort Sumter. From there, Teddy and I went to the nearest recruiting office and James set off to Washington D.C. That was the last time I ever saw him. At the recruiting office, we were both assigned to different units, as we were both accepted as officers, thus needed in different capacities. James had helped get us the appointments. After we left the recruiting office, I hugged Teddy goodbye, and we both went our separate ways. That was the last time I ever saw either of my brothers. I had not been home in nearly four years. All I wanted was to go home- now. I was hopeful that this detonation would be significant enough to end the war sooner than we all expected. I felt as if a part of me was missing. I had no brothers and no father. My poor mother must have been feeling devastated and lonely. It was truly ironic that they had both warned me to be safe, and now, I was the last one alive.

CHAPTER 22

12 July 1864, Petersburg, Virginia.

Progress on the mine beneath the rebels had been tremendous and brought a mere theory to reality. After a few weeks of back-breaking labor, the mine was near completion and the transport of thousands of pounds of gunpowder was imminent. Nobody thought we were going to get this far in the project. The thunder of artillery had not ceased once during the entire siege. We relentlessly bombarded the rebel lines for months, and they had not let up in the slightest. This detonation would hopefully alter the course of the war as it stood. I called a meeting of my brigade staff to discuss the upcoming operation.

"Gentlemen, as we know, this operation is

dangerous, risky, and hard-headed. Just the way we like it," I unfolded a map before them. "This is where the detonation will occur. A brigade will attack on either side, and we are to reinforce the one that needs it more. It is our discretion which way we go." I was drawing on the map with my pencil.

"Who will be embarking on the initial assault, sir?" asked a curious Major Stillwell.

"A specially trained division of Negroes under General Ferrero. They are aware of the composition of the job, and know exactly what to do," I answered with confidence.

"Very well," said the Major.

"Any more questions, gentlemen?" I asked the room,

"Sir, how will the brigade be divided? Who will take command where?" Lieutenant Baird asked. I began laughing.

"You boys haven't been here for very long, have you? I lead the brigade from the front. No dividing. That's the way I do things. You can't lead from the rear," I said with a straight face.

"Yes, sir." The men looked ghastly.

"Now, if there aren't any more questions, you should all start distributing your respective orders," I said as I passed out the papers and they exited the tent.

I spent the rest of the night thinking about the letter from the President. I was grateful for it, yet I felt besmirched. How was a Congressional Representative slain right damn near the capitol? I suppose Jubal Early's raids up north were successful. They were applying more pressure to Washington than we were to Richmond, and there were a hundred thousand of us there. His raids were putting the fear of God in the northern politicians, and would most likely interfere with the election in November. General Sheridan was dispatched to deal with the rebel force in the Shenandoah Valley and had been attempting to drive them out of there, and it had been mostly successful. I assumed a few stragglers tried to wreak havoc near the capitol the one night my brother decided to go for an ill-fated carriage ride. It was a truly unfortunate turn of events. There was nothing I could do about it, and I knew it. All I could do from here was kick the shit out of the rebels like I had been doing, and continue to do so.

CHAPTER 23

29 July 1864, Petersburg, Virginia.

The mine was completely finished and the last few hundred pounds of powder was being hauled in by our very own 69th New Jersey. I called a meeting with the brigade staff one more time before the big assault in the morning.

"Gentlemen, this is our last meeting before the big assault tomorrow," I said as the artillery bombardment grew twice as strong for the impending assault. "I need to know if we have any issues in the Brigade. Give me a complete list of numbers, supplies, anything I need to know before the morning," I said with a pale face.

"We are one-thousand and seven strong, all

the men have forty rounds of ammunition a piece. They are well-fed, and well-rested, save for the 69th, who will be by the morning," said a weary Captain Lowell, our quartermaster.

"Excellent. Does anyone have any last-minute questions before I see General Burnside?" I asked, as I was about to walk out.

"No sir. We have everything pretty well-covered," said Major Stillwell.

"Outstanding. I'll see you fellas in the morning." I briskly made my way to IX Corps headquarters. The flags were flying high as the streaks of smoke from huge siege cannons filled the once blue sky. I entered the headquarters to find Generals Meade and Burnside in a heated argument.

"That is a goddamn order, Burnside! I can't risk it! Those coloreds are not going to make this assault!" General Meade was reaming Burnside before Burnside fired back.

"I trained these men for this job! I'm not giving a task like this to some fresh hillbilly you found on the street!" General Meade was fuming.

"You bald, arrogant, scoundrel! You know damn well those are the men in your own damn Corps! That is an order, you shall obey it, damn you!" General Meade picked up his hat and bumped into me on the way out, completely dismissing me.

"God dammit. Now I have to find a new division to send across." He lit a cigar.

"What the hell just happened, sir?" I looked at him with genuine concern.

"I can't send in the USCT because of backlash from Northern newspapers in case this goes wrong, this close to the election. He's just cursed us by removing the group I specifically trained for this job." He looked down in disappointment.

"I could lead that assault, sir." I said as I stood up straight.

"You? You're just a brigade commander. What skill set do you offer that's different from them?" he said, raising an eyebrow.

"Your men will go in too, I'll just be the one to

lead the way. My men were built for this job, sir. Up close and personal, we'll run them through with the bayonet. Every engagement since Fredericksburg we've been the ones in the front with buck and ball giving the rebels what they had coming to them." I began to smile.

"I like you, son. You can lead the charge. I just need to pick a new goddamn division to go with you." He wrote me my orders.

"Yes sir, thank you sir." I saluted and exited the tent.

I quickly rushed back to my tent and furiously began writing my orders to regimental commanders.

"Stillwell! Get in here!" I shouted as I folded paper with ink still wet while out of breath from running.

"Take these new orders. We are leading the charge." I said with a smile. He smiled back.

"Yes, sir." He saluted and began distributing the orders.

This was our defining moment. This could be the moment that ends the largest conflict in history. The Bear Brigade would drive its claws through the line at Petersburg. It was just what I wanted. Joshua walked up to me.

"Willy, where are you going?" The grim reality of what was about to happen dawned on me.

"We're going into combat tomorrow, Joshua." I said, as I looked him in the eye.

"Will you come back?" His innocent eyes looked back at me. I didn't have the heart to lie.

"I don't know," I said as I looked down. He grabbed my arm.

"Either way, I'll still be here, waiting for you." He walked away to draw on my desk. He brought a tear to my eye.

CHAPTER 24

30 July 1864, Petersburg, Virginia.

General Burnside had selected General Ledlie and his division for the assault on the crater. General Ledlie was nowhere to be found, but his division was battle-ready. In his absence, I assumed command of his division and my brigade, courtesy of General Burnside. We were next to them as a Pennsylvania miner lit the fuse leading to the rebel lines. Just behind me was the battle-hungry Bear Brigade, eleven-hundred strong. We waited patiently for the huge explosion. I covered my ears as several minutes passed by, but nothing happened. A few more minutes passed by and still nothing. It was a pitch-dark morning with an eerie silence. A quiet voice piped up.

"The fuse went out. Someone has to go in and relight it," said an unknown soldier. It was a job that no one on the planet would envy. Before long, some of those brave Pennsylvania miners went in, relit the fuse, and covered the entrance with sandbags. I covered my ears again as the fuse got closer and closer. Before long, a colossal explosion rocked the earth, shaking everything and sending a shockwave in all directions. My ears were bleeding, and the ground was shaking. A shower of dirt, body parts, rifles, cannons, and bodies were sent soaring in all directions. Several minutes went by as nothing happened. No orders were being shouted, and no bugles were being sounded. I looked around, confused, before I finally took the reins.

"Come on men! Charge! Give them all you've got! Run around the crater and surround them boys!" I waved my sword in the air as I jumped over the top and was the first to set foot on no man's land. Soon, the first division and the Bear Brigade were right behind me. The batteries of artillery began shaking the ground once again as explosions rocked the already beleaguered and confused rebels. A relentless hellfire showered down on them, sending them into a panic. They had not returned fire yet, and we were nearly at the crater. Men of the first division began to run into the crater itself, rather than going around it.

"You damn fools! Get the hell out of there and run around!" I shouted, but to no avail.

Men were running into the crater and couldn't make their way out. They were sprinting in, and any man who fell down was instantly trampled to death where they laid. The Bear Brigade had halted behind me in a pristine formation as I watched in horror as the entire division was being slaughtered in the crater. None of them could make it out. Rebels had surrounded the crater and were pouring deadly musketry down on them in addition to canister shot, which was turning men into a repulsive liquid. In combination with the blood, guts, and mud, the crater was becoming something of a cursed bowl of soup. Before long, it was made worse, as General Burnside committed the division under General Ferrero to the attack. The black troops were sent in and met the same fate as Ledlie's first division. I turned to shout at the brigade.

"Spread out, independent fire on the rebels outside the crater! Try to cover those poor boys as best you can!" I shouted with a wide-eyed glare at the crater of bodies.

No one could make it out of the crater. The more men tried to writhe and crawl, the more they were mercilessly slaughtered. The Bear Brigade was returning fire as best it could, but it wasn't making a difference. The sun began to rise, revealing the true devastation surrounding the crater and the crater itself. A layer of guts paved the surrounding earth. Broken cannons, wood, fallen trees, planks, body parts, and rifles were scattered around the battlefield. The crater itself was becoming more full of corpses and awful soup. It was massive, over one-hundred feet in diameter, and over thirty feet deep. The air was dry before the attack. Now, it was humid with the evaporating blood and gore with every dying soldier. Artillery had worsened, making it even more impossible for either side to make any progress. As the movement in the crater began to slow to almost nothing, the rebels turned their attention to us. Soon, volleys began raining down on us in addition to devastating artillery. A few regiments of rebels had left their entrenchments to try and route us. I was not going to let that happen.

As they formed their battle lines, I ordered the Bear Brigade into battle formation. They lined up, three ranks deep, fixed bayonets, and took aim at the rebels.

"Ready!" I raised my sword. "Fire!" A crackle of musketry fell down the line, sending thousands of bullets into the rebels. Hundreds of them fell as we walked closer to them,

"Reload!" I shouted. "Take aim!" I raised my sword. "Fire!" Another massive crackle of fire was rippling down the line. The rebels had not fired back. Another hundred of them fell.

"Prepare to charge! Hold for my order!" I screamed as an eerie silence fell across the battlefield. I witnessed the rebels attempt to line up.

"Charge! Give no quarter, slaughter them all!" I ran in ahead of the boys as they followed close behind me. I ran in with the most fire and fury I had channeled during the war. A fire had taken over my eyes as I mercilessly slaughtered everything in my path. I didn't care how old, how young, if they were wounded or not. They took both of my brothers, so I would slaughter every last one of them until they had nothing left to send at us.

There were only about eight-hundred of them left standing. The entire brigade had committed themselves to the attack. We were keeping the rebels occupied as a few stragglers from the first division made it back to friendly lines. I watched men drown one another in other people's guts. There were limbs everywhere and the air was now filled with blood as if a monsoon was passing by. Soon, a rebel officer drew his sword and ran at me. It was a duel to the death. He had knocked the sword out of my hands, cutting my arm deep, causing a fountain of blood to spurt out of my arm. I punched him in the face with my good arm, knocking him to the ground. I kneeled on his neck, my knee on his throat, putting all my weight down on him. I raised my fist and relentlessly punched him until his face was reduced to a bloody pulp. I only stopped after men pulled me away from his lifeless corpse.

We reorganized and walked back to our lines. Our blue uniforms had been permanently stained red, much like General Burnside's reputation. Total casualties for the Battle of the Crater were well over four-thousand federals and only fifteen-hundred rebels. The attack was a dismal failure.

I slowly entered my quarters with a blank stare at the ground. Joshua looked up at me.

"Are you ok, Willy?" He had a concerned and frightened look on his face. I looked down at my bloodied uniform and back down at him.

"Never go to war, kid. It's never worth it." I fell to the ground, bleeding from the severe arm injury. Joshua ran up to me, tapping me frantically.

"Willy! Willy, are you ok! Don't go... I need you..." The voice faded into darkness.

◆ ◆ ◆

"If you see the President, tell him from me that whatever happens there will be no turning back." ~Ulysses S. Grant

EPILOGUE

Washington D.C.

General Burnside was responsible for one of the worst military disasters of the Civil War, his second to date behind Fredericksburg. General Ledlie was found hiding out in a bomb-proof shelter with General Ferrero, both drunk beyond their minds. After the Battle of the Crater, the Petersburg Siege had remained completely unchanged.

The siege ended in March of 1865. In the weeks following, the Confederate Army of Northern Virginia, under General Robert E. Lee, surrendered at Appomattox Court House on April 9, 1865. Joshua had stayed with the Bear Brigade throughout the siege and witnessed the surrender. The Bear Brigade was mustered out of service in May of 1865. Joshua's whereabouts after May of 1865 were unknown.

President Lincoln had defeated the Democratic nominee, General George McClellan, decisively and was inaugurated for a second term in office in early 1865. He had also passed the 13th Amendment, outlying slavery in the United States in early 1865. On April 14, 1865, President Abraham Lincoln was shot by Confederate sympathizer and famous actor, John Wilkes Booth. He died the following morning on April 15.

Ulysses S. Grant had effectively won the Civil War. After the Presidency of Andrew Johnson, Ulysses Grant was decidedly elected to two terms in office, beginning the Reconstruction Era. He had annihilated the first Ku Klux Klan, and passed the Civil Rights Act of 1871 becoming a hero to all, and one of the legendarily heroic figures in American History, beside Abraham Lincoln.

BOOKS BY THIS AUTHOR

High Horse: A Harrowing Story Of The Western Theater In The Bloodiest Conflict In American History

The compelling tale of an aspiring young officer that faces some of the most consequential decision making and events in United States History.

A Shot In The Dark: "A Sobering Story Of The Grim Reality Of Our American Civil War."

An intense insight into the wartime life of an old-fashioned artillery officer, who must learn the complexities of modern warfare during the American Civil War.

The Ultimate Resolution

A symbolic, literary representation of some of the

most intense moments during the First World War told through the lense of the United States Marine 'Devil Dogs' and 'The Lost Battalion'.

Made in the USA
Middletown, DE
14 May 2023

30153529R00080